GREAT ILLUSTRATED CLASSICS

THE ADVENTURES OF
ROBINSON CRUSOE

Daniel Defoe

adapted by
Malvina G. Vogel

BARONET
B·O·O·K·S

BARONET BOOKS, New York, New York

GREAT ILLUSTRATED CLASSICS

edited by
Malvina G. Vogel

CONTENTS

CHAPTER   PAGE

1. Robinson's Early Adventures 9
2. Shipwreck! 19
3. Starting a New Life 33
4. Robinson Learns Many Skills 47
5. Robinson Makes a Canoe 67
6. The Mysterious Footprint 85
7. Cannibals! 95
8. The First Sound of a Man's Voice .. 107
9. Friday 123
10. The Cannibals Return 145
11. Two Visitors 159
12. Englishmen Reach the Island 173
13. Robinson Puts Down a Mutiny 189
14. Robinson Seizes the Ship 207
15. Home Again 225

About the Author

Daniel Defoe was born in London in 1660. After many years of studying for the ministry, Daniel decided that a religious life did not suit him. He chose, instead, to become a merchant.

He traveled widely and built up a successful business. During this period, he married and started raising a family.

But in 1692, his business failed, leaving the 32-year-old Defoe heavily in debt, with a wife and six children to support. Since he had always been interested in politics, he tried making his living by writing political articles for newspapers. These articles often criticized the king and the ruling party. As a result, Defoe spent many years in and out of prison.

Since his political writings had brought only troubles and increasing debts, Defoe turned to fiction writing. His first novel, written in 1719 when Defoe was nearly sixty years old, was to become one of the best known adventure stories in the world. That novel was *Robinson Crusoe*—a story which still thrills readers today, more than two hundred fifty years later.

Robinson Crusoe brought Defoe great success and helped him pay back part of his debts. He continued writing novels such as *Moll Flanders, Colonel Jack,* and two other Robinson Crusoe stories, but his creditors always seemed to be one step behind him.

During his last years, Defoe was a sick, lonely old man, hunted by his creditors and abandoned by his ungrateful children. He died in 1731 at the age of seventy-one, as alone and frightened as his hero, Robinson, had been during his twenty-eight years on a deserted island.

ATLANTIC OCEAN

CARIBBEAN SEA

ORINOCO R.

AMAZON R.

SOUTH AMERICA

Robinson's Island

Characters You Will Meet

Robinson Crusoe, *a merchant seaman cast ashore on an uninhabited island*

Friday, *a young native who becomes Robinson Crusoe's faithful servant*

The Spaniard, *a prisoner of the cannibals*

Friday's Father, *another prisoner of the cannibals who is rescued by his own son*

The Captain, *the captain of a ship which comes to the island*

A Warning

Chapter 1
Robinson's Early Adventures

"Robinson, if you go to sea, your life will be one of misery," said Mr. Crusoe, "and you will live to regret it!"

But eighteen-year-old Robinson Crusoe was not moved by his father's words or by the old man's tears. The only thing he wanted in life was to go to sea to make his fortune. He didn't want to study law as his father had hoped. He didn't want to share in his family's successful business as his mother had hoped.

"Just one voyage," argued Robinson, "and if I do not like it, I shall return and stay here with the family in Yorkshire."

But Mr. and Mrs. Crusoe would not give their consent. A sailor's life was a dangerous one. Storms were regular occurrences at sea. Their winds often blew ships off course and, even worse, dashed them to pieces against rocks or sand bars. Many lives were lost this way. Then, too, there was the danger of pirates who attacked merchant ships, stole their cargo, and killed their crew. No, Mr. and Mrs. Crusoe decided, they could not give their consent and be part of the destruction of their son.

So, for another year, Robinson could only dream of going to sea. One day, he was visiting a friend in the seaport town of Hull. Robinson learned that the boy's father, a sea captain, was setting sail on a short voyage down the English coast to London. An invitation to come on board and sail as the captain's guest was too much for Robinson to resist.

Danger at Sea

So, on the first of September, in the year 1651, Robinson Crusoe began the first of many adventures which would take him to Africa, to South America, and to an island in the Caribbean Sea before he ever returned to English soil again.

On his first voyage, Robinson learned what it was like to be violently seasick when his ship was caught in a storm. He learned how fierce and destructive a storm at sea could be, and how he felt being at the mercy of raging waves and driving winds.

But all the fear and the seasickness were soon forgotten once Robinson was rescued and returned to dry land. Soon after that, he set sail on his second voyage, this time to the coast of Africa. He learned how to become a successful trader with the natives. He learned the terror of being attacked and captured by a band of pirates. He learned the misery of life as a slave to the pirate captain

Robinson is Seasick.

and the joy of escaping in the captain's smal
fishing boat.

When Robinson was finally rescued from
the sea, it was by a Portuguese merchant shij
heading to the South American country o
Brazil. In Brazil, Robinson went to work on a
sugar plantation and, after several years, he
bought a plantation of his own. He ran hi
plantation successfully for several years and
made many friends among the other planters

When the planters realized that they need
ed extra help to run their plantations, the
asked Robinson if he would make a voyage to
Africa to buy slaves for them. The Africar
natives made very good, loyal workers. Be
sides, Robinson had been to Africa before and
knew how to trade with the natives.

Yet, he had a very successful plantatior
built up over the years. To leave it now and
go on such a dangerous voyage across the At
lantic Ocean might seem foolish or mad. Bu

Robinson's Sugar Plantation

the idea of another sea voyage excited Robinson so, that he agreed to go.

The other planters promised to take care of Robinson's plantation while he was gone and also to follow the instructions in his will if he did not return.

So, on the first of September, in the year 1659—eight years to the day he boarded his first ship at Hull, England—Robinson Crusoe set sail from San Salvador, Brazil. This voyage was to become the greatest adventure of his or any man's lifetime!

The Plantation Will Be Cared For.

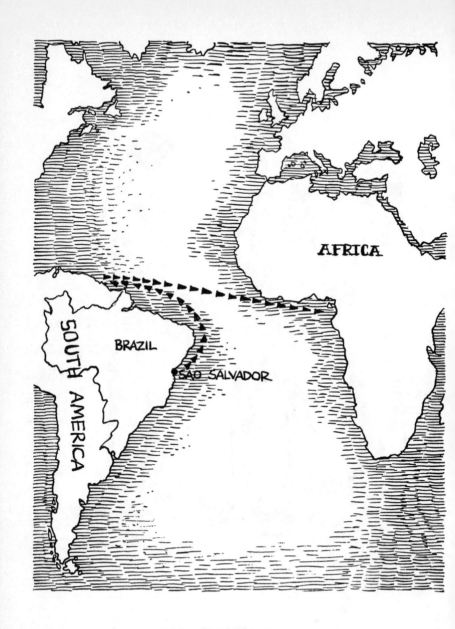

The Ship's Course

Chapter 2
Shipwreck!

The ship sailing out of São Salvador that sunny September morning carried fourteen men aboard: its captain, twelve sailors, and Robinson Crusoe. As cargo she carried toys which Robinson planned to use in his trade with the natives. These toys included beads, shells, knives, scissors, hatchets, and small mirrors.

The captain set the ship's course to the north, along the Brazilian coast. Then he planned to head east across the Atlantic Ocean to reach their destination in Africa.

On their twelfth day at sea, as they were nearing the northern tip of South America, a violent hurricane struck. For ten straight days, the fury of the winds pushed the ship in every direction. Two men were washed overboard, and one died of a tropical fever. From moment to moment, Robinson expected to be swallowed up by the sea. Sails were ripped, masts were broken, and the ship was leaking in several places.

By the eleventh day, when the winds had died down, Robinson and the captain examined the damage. They agreed that the ship was in no condition to continue on to Africa. The captain wanted to return to Brazil, but Robinson disagreed. They were so far north already, it would be closer to head for one of the British islands in the Caribbean Sea. The island of Barbados was only a fifteen-day sail. They could repair the ship there.

Damage from the Hurricane

But a second storm hit and pulled them off course again. The strong currents were pulling them east, towards land inhabited by uncivilized savages.

The ship was battered about by the winds and the sea all night long. At dawn, Robinson was awakened in his cabin by the cries of "Land! Land!" He ran up on deck to see where the lookout was pointing.

But, at that moment, the ship gave a lurch as it struck a sand bar and stopped dead. The sea continued to batter the crippled ship with all its force. As the wind increased, Robinson wondered how much more punishment his ship could take before she broke apart. There was nothing left now but to abandon ship, so the captain gave the orders.

The crew immediately began lowering the one lifeboat they carried, and everyone piled in. The winds had calmed down a little, but the sea was rising higher and higher. The

Lowering the Lifeboat

lifeboat had no sail, so the men rowed with all their might. But they were at the mercy of the wild sea.

Suddenly, a raging wave over thirty feet high came at them from the stern. There wasn't a moment for the eleven men even to take a breath before the wave overturned the boat and swallowed them all up.

Although Robinson was a good swimmer, he couldn't fight the force of the mighty wave. He sank below the surface and let the wave carry his nearly lifeless body wherever it chose.

It drove him towards the shore and left him partway there, half dead with the water he had swallowed. He tried to touch bottom with his feet before the next wave came, but, before he could manage it, he found himself buried again in thirty feet of water and carried swiftly towards shore. This time, at least, Robinson was able to hold his breath.

The Raging Wave

But just as he felt his lungs ready to burst, his head and hands shot above the surface of the water.

As the pull of the sea tried to drag him back out again, Robinson dug his feet into the sand. But the sea was not done with him yet. Twice more, he was lifted up by the waves and carried in. The last wave dashed him against a large rock with such force that the air was nearly crushed out of his body.

With a last burst of strength, Robinson got to his feet and ran to shore. There, out of reach of the brutal waves, he collapsed on the sand.

After he had vomited out the salt water from his stomach, he lay there gasping for air, trying to catch his breath. As his strength gradually returned, Robinson said a prayer of thanks to God for saving his life. Every single one of his crew had drowned, but his life had been spared.

Safe on Shore

He sat up and looked out to his stranded ship. It was so far out, he began to wonder how he had ever made it to shore.

When he felt strong enough to stand up and look around him, Robinson's joy immediately turned to sadness. He was alone here. But where was *here?* He had nothing to eat or drink. Would he die of hunger? Or would he be attacked and eaten by some wild beasts? He had no weapons with which to hunt or defend himself other than a small knife in his belt.

These fears hit him so suddenly that he began running about the shore like a madman, beating his chest and screaming to God, "Why have You saved me only to make me suffer in this misery?"

When he had no more strength to run or scream, Robinson sat down on the sand and tried to clear his thoughts. Night was coming on, but before the light was gone completely,

The Stranded Ship

he had to find some fresh water to drink. So he walked a little ways inland and found a small stream with cool fresh water.

Next, he had to find a place for himself for the night—a place where he would be protected from an attack by wild beasts. He found a large, thick, fir-like tree and climbed up into it. As he tried to make himself comfortable on two strong branches, his mind was filled with thoughts of what kind of death he would die the next day.

But in spite of these thoughts, Robinson was so exhausted that he soon fell asleep.

Exhaustion!

The Ship Drifted In.

Chapter 3
Starting a New Life

When Robinson awoke the next morning, the weather was clear. The storm had passed. He pushed aside the thick branches of the tree and looked out towards the calm sea. He was surprised to see that his ship had loosened from the sand bar during the night and had drifted in with the tide. She now lay against the rocks a quarter of a mile from shore.

"How sad!" cried Robinson. "If only my men had stayed aboard, they might be alive now." But Robinson's tears could not help them now. Nor could they help him either. He had to get out to the ship and take off whatever might be useful to him here on the island.

By noon, the tide was so far out and the sea so shallow that Robinson had no difficulty swimming out to the ship. He grabbed onto a rope hanging down from the deck, climbed aboard, and began his search.

Luck was with him, for all of the ship's food was dry and untouched by the salt water. Since he had had nothing to eat since yesterday, Robinson began stuffing his mouth, then his pockets with biscuits. But there was more to be taken off the ship besides food, and, in order to get everything ashore, he would need a boat.

Robinson found some spare masts which would make a good raft. He tied each one with a rope and began tossing them over the side into the sea. He held the ends of the ropes so the masts wouldn't float away. Then

Robinson Climbs on Board.

he climbed down himself and began lashing the masts together.

After several hours, Robinson was able to start loading his raft. First, he piled on all the loose boards he could find. On top of these, he placed an empty seaman's chest and filled it with food: bread, rice, cheese, dried meat, corn, and some bottles of rum. He covered these provisions with some extra clothes for himself, since his own were now in rags from the pounding of the sea.

Next, he turned his attention to the tools he'd need on shore. He found the carpenter's chest filled with saws, axes, and hammers, and got these down to his raft too.

But he would need arms and ammunition as well if he hoped to hunt for his food and, if necessary, defend himself against man or beast. He found several muskets, three good shotguns, two pistols, and an old rusty sword. A barrel of gunpowder and a bag of bullets

Loading the Raft

completed his take.

By the time everything was loaded on th
raft, the tide had begun to rise and head i
towards shore. The tide, plus the wind, car
ried him along until he felt himself caught u
in a strong current. He was being pulle
away from the place where he had first en
tered the water.

Robinson knew that currents like this ofte
occurred when there was a creek or rive
nearby. He hoped that this was so, for i
would be easier to land his raft along a cree
than push it up on the beach.

Robinson was delighted when he spotted a
deep creek and felt the current pull his raf
into it. A little way along, he spied a smal
cove on one of the banks. It was perfect! Dee
enough to land the raft and still close enoug
to the sea for Robinson to watch for a passin
ship.

Once on shore, with his raft safely tied to

Robinson Finds the Creek.

tree, Robinson headed for a steep hill. From the top, he hoped to get a good view of the land around him. Was it an island? Was it the coast of the mainland? He had no way of knowing.

Robinson climbed to the top and discovered that the sea surrounded him on all sides. He was on an island, and there was no land any-where, as far as his eye could see.

So he returned to the bank of the creek and set up a hut for himself from the boards that lay on his raft. Then he lay down inside it to rest.

But Robinson's mind was not ready to rest just yet. He had to plan ahead and decide what to do next. First, he had to return to the ship for other supplies. And he had to do it soon, for if another storm hit, it would eas-ily break the ship to pieces. Then all would be lost.

So Robinson decided that before he did

Robinson's First Hut

anything else on the island, he would return to the ship as many times as necessary to take off whatever might be of value to him.

Every day, for the next three weeks, Robinson went out to the ship. He brought back bags of nails, hatchets, crowbars, scissors, knives, forks, and a stone to sharpen his tools. He also brought a compass, maps, a spyglass, more clothing, blankets, sails, ropes, canvas, and even some coins of gold and silver. Then he added four companions for himself: the ship's dog, two cats, and a Bible.

The fourth week began with a raging, stormy night. The following morning, Robinson looked out to sea. The ship was nowhere to be seen. Only bits of a wreck stuck up out of the water at low tide.

Now that he was on shore to stay, Robinson began to search for a place to build his home. The place had to be close to fresh water; it

More Supplies for Shore

had to have some kind of shade from the sun; it had to be safe from wild creatures, either man or beast; and it had to have a good view of the sea. For Robinson still hoped for a passing ship to rescue him.

So Robinson started his search. As the days passed, he realized that he had to have some way to keep a record of the time he was spending on the island. Since he had no paper or pen or ink, he set up a large post near the shore, and each day, he cut a notch into it. Every seventh day, he cut a longer notch through the six notches, and so marked off a week, then a month, and then a year.

Robinson's Calendar Post

Robinson Builds His Home.

Chapter 4
Robinson Learns Many Skills

Robinson's days of searching for a place to build his home ended when he found a small flat plain on the side of a hill. There was even a spot worn away in the side of the hill that looked like the beginning of a cave. It was on the flat plain in front of this spot that Robinson decided to settle.

He pitched his tent, using some of the sails he had taken from the ship. Then for protection he built himself a fortress surrounding it. The fortress was made of strong young trees which Robinson chopped down and cut

47

into points at the tips. He drove these into the ground, pointed tips up, in a half-circle around his tent. So his fortress began at one side of the hill and ran to the other, enclosing his tent and all his possessions. To get inside his fortress, Robinson built a ladder, which he then pulled in after him.

Once his fortress was finished, Robinson began to dig out the earth and rock from the side of the hill to make himself a cave. He needed a cool, dry place where he would be protected from the sun and rain and where he could store his provisions.

Even while he was putting his home in order, Robinson made sure to go out every day to hunt for food. He found many ducks, pigeons, goats, and turtles on the island. The meat they provided, plus the goats' milk and the turtles' eggs, became the basis of Robinson's food supply. When he killed an animal whose meat was not good for eating, he took

The Fortress

off its skin, dried it, and used it for clothing or covering.

Robinson's home was now ready to be furnished. But what could a man who had never handled a tool in his life hope to build? Robinson wasn't sure, but he worked patiently with his axe and saw for months. At first he pulled apart everything he made. But finally, he developed enough skill to make himself a table and a chair, then some shelves for his cave.

Once Robinson had succeeded as a carpenter, he decided to try his hand at farming. He still had the kernels of barleycorn he had taken off the ship. This would be his first crop.

He found a flat, clear piece of land which had to be dug up and plowed. Since an iron spade was not one of the tools a ship carried Robinson had to make himself one. And the only material he had available was wood. He

Robinson Becomes a Carpenter.

found a tree whose wood was quite hard, and even though this wood was difficult to work with, Robinson managed to shape a board into the spade he needed. Therefore, he was able to dig up the ground and plant his crop.

But this first crop never grew, for Robinson had planted it at the wrong time of the year—just before the dry season. Since he had only used half his kernels on this first planting, he still had the other half left. His second crop, planted just before the rainy season, sprouted and grew well.

Robinson carefully saved every ear of corn when it was ripe. He had to think of replanting and increasing his crop before he could think about making bread from his grain. Bread was not to come until much later, three years to be exact.

By the time Robinson had been on the island ten months, he decided to explore the creek as it traveled inland. Along its banks

The Second Corn Crop Grows.

he discovered fields of wild tobacco and sugar cane, vines of sweet ripe grapes, and trees covered with oranges lemons, and limes. Of these fruits, the most valuable to him turned out to be the grapes. While all the other fruits had to be eaten soon after picking before they spoiled, the grapes could be hung in bunches from any tree's branches and dried in the sun. Once they dried and became raisins, they could be kept for long periods of time without spoiling. Not only were they tasty, but they were very nourishing as well.

The grapes proved especially valuable to Robinson during the rainy season when he was unable to leave his cave or tent for several weeks. When there was a slight break in the weather, he left his home only to kill a goat or turtle which roamed nearby. But the fresh fruits grew too far inland to reach during the rainy weather.

By the time 365 notches were cut into

Drying Grapes into Raisins

Robinson's calendar post, he had learned when to expect the rainy and dry seasons on the island. This was important in the planting of his crops in order to yield two harvests each year for himself. He found that the seasons of the year were not divided into winter and summer as they were in England, but into rainy, dry, rainy, dry. Knowing what to expect helped Robinson store up his supplies so he would not have to go out too much during the wet months.

While he was indoors, he busied himself with enlarging his cave and weaving baskets out of long, thin twigs. These baskets were useful for storing his corn and raisins, as well as for carrying out the earth and rock from his cave.

During his second year, Robinson made many trips exploring the island. On one trip, he climbed a high hill—the highest he had found so far. The day was very clear, and off

Weaving Baskets

to the west, about forty miles, Robinson spied land. He didn't know if it was another island or the mainland. He didn't know if it was inhabited or not. But he did know that if there were inhabitants, they were savages. For while he lived in Brazil, Robinson had heard stories about the savages who inhabited this part of the world. They were cannibals, man-eaters who killed and ate all human beings who fell into their hands. The thought of cannibals made Robinson shudder, and he thanked God that he had landed on this deserted island instead of among the cannibals.

During another one of his trips, Robinson found a flock of parrots. He decided to catch one and try to teach it to speak. This he did, although it took Old Polly four years to learn to call, "Robin Crusoe! Robin Crusoe!"

And so, the second year ended, and the third year began. Robinson's crops were now large enough so that he did not have to use

Old Polly

all of them for replanting. He could now begin to think about making his corn into bread. But he had to do a great deal of thinking first, for he had no mill to grind the corn into meal, no sieve to strain it, no jars in which to store it, and no oven in which to bake it.

First, he began by experimenting with some clay he dug up on the island. He mixed it with water to form a paste, then shaped the paste into jars, and set the jars out in the sun to dry. His first few jars were ugly, misshapen things that either cracked to pieces while drying or caved in from their own weight.

After two months of experimenting, Robinson succeeded in making several small earthenware bowls, dishes, pots, and pitchers. But the two large earthen things he made were so ugly that he would not even call them jars.

Making Pottery

Now that he had a place to store the mea
once it was ground, Robinson had to fin
some sort of stone on which to grind his cor
into meal. The only stone on the island wa
very soft and crumbled easily, so tha
wouldn't do. Instead, he cut a block from th
same hard wood he had used for his spade
then hollowed out the inside. Next, he mad
a pestle or beater to mash the corn and foun
that it worked very well.

Now the meal had to be separated from th
husk or shell. Robinson had no sieve o
strainer with which to do this and no thi
cloth to take its place. Then he remembered
neckerchief he had taken from one of th
chests on the ship. By pulling out some of it
threads, he managed to make a strainer tha
accomplished the job of separating the hus
from the meal.

Then came the problem of baking th
bread. Robinson had no oven, but he did hav

Mashing the Corn

a clever mind. He hit upon the idea of making two very large earthenware pans. He put his bread in one pan, then covered it with the other. He set his covered pan onto half the coals in a red-hot fire. Then he piled the rest of the coals on top of the pan and around its sides. His bread then began to bake.

So, by the end of his third year on the island, Robinson Crusoe had added baking to the skills he had already learned—hunting, farming, and carpentry.

Baking Bread

The Mysterious Land Across the Sea

Chapter 5
Robinson Makes a Canoe

Even though Robinson was in his fourth year on the island, he had never forgotten the glimpse of land he had caught two years before while he was exploring the western shore.

His home was built and his crops were growing well. Robinson now had time to think about a voyage to that mysterious land across the sea. Perhaps it just might lead to an escape for him!

So Robinson decided to build a boat. He remembered that the natives in Brazil had made canoes from the trunks of large trees. He would try it too.

He found a large cedar tree whose trunk was six feet thick. It took him twenty days just to chop it down and another fourteen days to cut away its branches. Then he spent a month shaping the bottom so it would float and three months clearing out the inside with a hammer and an axe.

At the end of five months, Robinson had a boat big enough to fit twenty men. He was delighted with his work. But he hadn't considered before he started how he would get his boat to water.

The boat lay one hundred yards from the creek, but it might as well have been one hundred miles. The boat was too heavy for one man to push. So Robinson was forced to give up the idea of launching his boat. But he did learn a lesson from his five months of work. That lesson was to plan ahead before

Building a Boat

beginning any other project. If he ever built another boat, it would be much smaller and lighter, and it would be built much closer to the water.

Robinson turned his attention next to his clothing. Four years of living in the same pants and shirts he had taken off the ship had worn them into rags. Even though there was no real need to wear clothing in such a hot climate—especially since there were no other people around—still Robinson could not bring himself to walk around naked. The heat of the sun often burned and blistered his skin and gave him such headaches that he had to wear pants, a shirt, and a cap at all times.

But as his clothes were now rotting, Robinson had to try making new ones. The only material he had to work with was the skins of animals he had caught. He stretched these skins and dried them in the sun. Those that

Drying Animal Skins

stayed soft, like goat skins, could be shaped and sewn into garments. First, he made a high cap with a flap hanging down over his neck in the back. The fur on the outside kept him dry during the heavy rains and kept the hot sun from burning his head and neck.

Seeing that this worked so well, Robinson tried making himself a suit of clothes out of these skins. He made a loose waistcoat—a kind of long vest—and pants down to his knees. He held everything together with a goatskin belt. But this belt also served another purpose, for he was able to hang his saw and hatchet from it. A second belt, this one slung over his shoulder, gave him a place to tie his pouches of gunpowder. To complete his outfit, Robinson made himself a pair of something which looked like laced sock boots.

Considering that he was no tailor, just as he had been no farmer or hunter or carpenter, Robinson was quite proud of his new

Robinson Makes New Clothes.

clothes. They fit fairly well, kept him dr
when it rained, and made him look like som
fierce, frightening creature. Not that ther
was anyone on the island to frighten!

Next, Robinson set about making himsel
an umbrella. The need for protection fror
the hot sun as well as from the heavy rain
made an umbrella necessary. After two o
three failures, Robinson finally managed t
make an umbrella from branches covere
with goatskin. It opened and closed easily s
he could carry it about with him.

At the end of his fifth year on the islanc
Robinson decided to try making anothe
canoe. His first one lay where he had built i
and served as a reminder to him to be wise
this time.

Robinson had learned his lesson well, an
his second canoe was smaller and lay close t
the water. This time he had no probler
launching it. Although the canoe was not bi

A Fine Umbrella

enough to take him on a voyage across the sea to the land he had seen, it was certainly big enough to take him on a tour around his island.

Robinson fitted out a little mast and made a sail out of some pieces left over from his ship's sails. He then built a locker on one side of the boat to store his food, his gun, and his ammunition. The locker would protect them from the sun, the rain, and the spray of the sea.

Then Robinson fastened his umbrella to the stern of the boat where it would serve as an awning for him as he sailed.

After several test sails in the creek, Robinson was ready to try his canoe in the sea. His sixth year was beginning as he set sail towards the east. Ahead of him lay a great ledge of rocks stretching out about six miles into the sea. Past the rocks, a sand bar extended out about another three miles. This

Robinson's New Boat

presented a problem. It meant that Robinson would have to sail at least nine miles out to sea to get around the rocks and the sand bar. He wasn't sure how well his canoe would do that far out to sea.

So Robinson pulled in to shore just before the rocks and tied up his boat. He climbed a hill which overlooked the sea. From this high place, Robinson was able to get a better view of the sea around him. With the help of his spyglass, he discovered a furious current beyond the rocks and sand bar. Robinson feared that if he tried to sail around them, he would be caught up in the current and carried so far out to sea that he would never be able to return to shore again.

But Robinson Crusoe was a daring sailor. He would fight the current!

And for many hours, that is exactly what he did. The current was more violent than he expected, and no amount of paddling with his

Fighting the Current

oars could fight it. After five hours, just when he thought his arms would drop from his shoulders, Robinson felt a breeze come up and push him away from the current. But he had no way of knowing in which direction he was being pushed. He could no longer see the island, and he had not brought his compass with him.

But the clouds that had been overhead all day finally broke up, and the sun shone through. Its position in the sky told Robinson he was heading north.

With the wind blowing, Robinson could now spread his sail and be carried along. After several hours, the northern shore of the island came into view and Robinson was able to land.

After he had eaten and slept a while, Robinson had to figure out how to get back to his side of the island. It was too risky to attempt it in his canoe the way he had come.

Sailing Along the Northern Shore

But going back on the west side of the island might be dangerous as well, since he had no way of knowing what the sea was like there.

So he decided to pull his canoe up on land, tie it securely, and return home on foot. Even though he hated to be without the canoe after all his months of hard work, Robinson simply wasn't interested in any more exciting adventures for the moment.

So, taking only his gun and his umbrella, Robinson began his long march along the shore towards home.

Returning Home on Foot

Trapping Goats

Chapter 6
The Mysterious Footprint

Robinson spent the next five years living a very quiet life. By his eleventh year, his gunpowder was beginning to run low. He had used it only for hunting. But how would he hunt when it was used up?

He decided to set up traps and try to capture enough goats to tame and breed for his food. His first trap, a pit in the ground, snared three young goats, a male and two females.

In about a year and a half, he had a flock of twelve goats, and in two years, forty-three.

Now that he had a tamed flock, Robinso
realized that he could get milk as well a
meat from them.

Robinson had never milked a cow in hi
life, and certainly not a goat. And he had n
idea how butter and cheese were made. Bu
after a great many trials and errors, he mar
aged to learn to do both.

Seven years had now passed since Robinso
had beached his canoe on the northern side o
the island. He was becoming impatient t
finish the voyage he had started. He had t
bring his canoe back!

So Robinson set off along the shore, plar
ning to walk east, then north. When h
reached the hill overlooking the rocks an
the sand bar, he saw that the sea was smoot
and quiet. There was no sign of the violer
current he had been caught in years befor
Why had it changed? Then Robinson realize
that the tide was out. That was it! He woul

The Violent Current is Gone.

be able to sail back through here as long as he did it when the tide was out, for when it returned to shore, the current started up again.

Overjoyed at this discovery, Robinson climbed down the hill and returned to the shore. He hadn't taken more than five steps in the sand when he stopped dead in his tracks. There, in front of him, in a place where he hadn't yet stepped, was a man's footprint!

Robinson stood stunned for several minutes. It was a human print. It had toes, a heel, and every part of a foot. And it was too large to be his own.

Robinson looked around and listened. Nothing! He climbed back up the hill and looked further. Still nothing! He ran up and down the shore, but he saw nobody there and no other print.

Putting aside all thoughts of his canoe, a

A Mysterious Footprint!

terrified Robinson turned and hurried home. With every step, he glanced behind him, imagining that every tree and every bush was a man. He didn't dare relax until he was safe inside his fortress.

There was no sleep for Robinson that night. His head was filled with thoughts that the Devil had come for him. For how would any human thing get to the island? There was no sign of any boat! And why weren't there any other footprints?

Then another, even more frightening, thought occurred to him. Perhaps a group of savages from the mainland had been driven to the island by the current. Perhaps they had found his boat and were looking for him right now. They would surely kill him and then eat him!

For three days and three nights, Robinson did not stir out of his fortress. Finally, his courage began to return and he thought more

Robinson Rushes Home in Fear.

clearly. He had been living on the island now for fifteen years. In all that time, he had not seen any sign of human life. Why, then, should he let a little thing like a footprint worry him?

Robinson tried very hard to talk himself out of his fears. Still, just to be prepared, he decided to strengthen his fortress. He added a second wall of thick stakes around the first wall and placed the seven muskets from the ship into openings between the stakes.

It took Robinson a month to build this second wall, and even when he was finished, he was still uneasy. He was still fearful of falling into the hands of savage cannibals.

Little did Robinson realize that his fears were real. There *was* danger of an attack by these savages!

Strengthening His Fortress

Was It a Boat?

Chapter 7
Cannibals!

For the next two years, Robinson kept away from the eastern end of the island where he had seen the footprint. He decided, instead, to explore the western end, which he had seen only once along the shore.

As he reached the top of a hill overlooking the sea, he thought he saw a boat far out in the distance. But he didn't have his spyglass with him, so he couldn't be sure. Within minutes, though, the boat was out of sight.

As Robinson turned his attention away from the sea and headed down the hill, he stopped dead in his tracks, more horrified than he had ever been in his life.

"Oh, my God!" he gasped as he saw hands, skulls, feet, and other bones of human bodies scattered in the sand. Nearby were the remains of a fire.

"The savages have been here," he cried, "and they have had a bloody feast on the bodies of their fellow human beings!"

Robinson turned away from this horrible sight. He grew sick to his stomach and felt faint. He soon began vomiting uncontrollably.

After several minutes, when the vomiting had stopped, Robinson turned and ran up the hill as fast as his legs would carry him. He didn't stop running until he was safely inside his fortress where he swore never to return to the western end of the island again.

For the next two years, whenever Robinson went out of his fortress, he used more caution and stayed more alert than he had ever done

"The Savages Have Been Here!"

before. He even stopped firing his gun fo
fear that any savages who might be on the is
land would hear it. Robinson was mor
thankful than ever that he had tamed hi
goats and was not forced to hunt in th
woods. But even though he didn't fire hi
gun, he kept it with him at all times, alon
with his pistols and his sword.

During those long months, Robinson's fea
gradually turned to anger. He began makin
plans for an attack on the savages if he eve
caught them at their bloody feasts. Man
wild schemes crossed his mind, but non
seemed very sound. He would be one ma
against twenty or thirty savages whose bow
and arrows were just as deadly and just a
accurate as his guns.

But the more he thought about the attack
the more he began questioning himself.

"Do I have the right to judge and murde
these people? I may consider them criminal

Armed at All Times

yet they are only doing what their people have been doing for years. Perhaps they do not consider eating human flesh a sin, just as I do not consider eating the flesh of a goat a sin.

"Then too," Robinson continued, "these people have done me no harm. They did not come to the island to attack me. So, why should I attack them? I might kill two or three cannibals, maybe even five or six. But if the rest of them escape, they might return with hundreds of others to kill me and eat me just to avenge the deaths of their countrymen."

So Robinson finally decided that if he saw the cannibals again, the wisest thing to do would be to hide. That way, they would never guess that another human being was on the island.

Still, the fear of constant danger did not leave Robinson. He went out from his fortress

"Why Should I Attack Them?"

only for necessary reasons. He no longer thought about building new things to make his life easier for fear that the banging of a nail or the chopping of wood would be heard. He even stopped making fires out of doors and did his cooking inside his cave for fear the smoke would give him away. The only thing that was important now was his safety, even more important than food.

Robinson had been on the island for twenty-three years. Four years had passed since he had made his bloody discovery. In those four years, there was no sign of any more visits by the cannibals. Robinson was almost convinced that no other savages would ever come here to disturb him again.

But in December of his twenty-third year, Robinson's peaceful life was disturbed. Early one morning, he spied some smoke rising from the shore on his side of the island. He placed his ladder up against the side of the

Smoke!

hill above his fortress and climbed to the top. He lay down on his stomach, and with his spyglass, he began to search for the fire.

The round circle of the glass soon revealed nine savages sitting around a small fire. But they soon got into their canoes and rowed away.

As soon as they were out of sight, Robinson grabbed his guns and headed for the beach. Blood, bones, and pieces of human flesh lay on the sand. Robinson's old murderous feelings returned, and he swore to destroy the savages the next time they set foot on the island.

Robinson Spies Savages.

A Ship Aground

Chapter 8
The First Sound of a Man's Voice

For the next year, Robinson thought about nothing but escaping from the island. By now, he longed for somebody to speak to, somebody to tell him where he was, and somebody to rescue him.

His hopes for rescue had been so high a few months earlier when a Spanish ship ran aground on the rocks. But when Robinson went for his boat and sailed out to the ship, he found only dead bodies and a small amount of cargo which he brought ashore.

The muskets, gunpowder, and clothing

would be of some use to him. And the only survivor, the ship's dog, would take the place of his first pet who had died many years earlier.

But how useless were the bags of gold he had found! They couldn't buy him another human being to talk to.

The idea of escape was now becoming so strong that Robinson could no longer resist it. He thought about it during the day and dreamed about it at night. The same dream kept repeating itself over and over, night after night. In the dream, the savages came to the island with a prisoner. The prisoner escaped from the savages and ran to Robinson for help. Robinson took him in, hid him, and soon had a faithful servant. This prisoner, a native, would help him escape to the mainland.

This dream became so real that Robinson decided there was only one way for him to es-

Robinson Dreams of Escape.

cape and that was to rescue one of the pris
oners the savages brought with them. Then
the rest of his dream would come true.

So, Robinson began his watch on the shore
He watched for six months; he watched for
year; he watched for a year and a half. Still
no canoes appeared on the sea.

Then, one morning, in his twenty-fifth yea
on the island, Robinson awoke and found th
canoes he had been searching for. There wer
five of them pulled up on the shore on h
side of the island. The savages who had bee
in them had already landed and were out c
sight. But five canoes could mean twenty c
thirty men! How could Robinson attack ther
singlehandedly?

He climbed to the top of the hill above h
fortress and saw thirty men dancing aroun
a fire. Their meat was cooking, but Robinso
couldn't be sure what meat it was.

As he watched, he saw two men bein

The Savages Return.

dragged from the boats towards the fire. One of them was immediately knocked down with a club, and the cannibals began cutting him open.

The other prisoner was left standing by himself until they were ready for him. Seeing himself unguarded and hoping to save his life, the native suddenly jumped away from them and ran into the woods. He was heading in Robinson's direction.

As Robinson gazed at these events, he couldn't help but wonder, "Can my dream be coming true?" Then he turned his attention back to the savages and saw that only three of them were sent after the fleeing native.

Robinson cheered silently as he saw the native outrunning the savages. "Keep running, my man!" he whispered. "You'll make it."

Then the native came to the creek. "Please, God," prayed Robinson, "let the man swim,

Is Robinson's Dream Coming True?

let him swim well and swiftly!"

The man dove in and, with strong, swift strokes, made it across the creek in seconds. When the three savages reached the creek, only two of them seemed to know how to swim. The third could not, so he turned and went back towards the beach.

The two savages were not as swift as the native, so he was well ahead of them by the time they reached the other side of the creek.

At this moment, Robinson knew that it was his fate to save the poor native's life. He ran down his ladder and grabbed his guns. He climbed over his fortress and took a shortcut to the creek.

Within minutes, Robinson stood just ten feet behind the fleeing native. He called out to him. The man turned and stared at Robinson. Robinson waved to him, calling him to come back, but the native was too frightened to move.

Robinson Calls to the Frightened Native.

Soon Robinson heard the savages approaching. He didn't want to fire his gun and warn the others, so he knocked the first savage out with the gun's butt end.

When the second savage saw his partner attacked, he pulled out his bow and arrow. There was no time to club him now, so Robinson fired. The savage fell dead.

The frightened native stared at his enemies on the ground. He was so terrified of the fire and the noise from Robinson's gun that he couldn't move.

Robinson called to him again and made signs for him to come closer. The man started walking, trembling, with each step. As he came closer, he began kneeling on the ground every ten or twelve steps. This was his way of thanking Robinson for having saved his life.

Robinson smiled at him. The man came closer, and when he reached Robinson, he

Attacking the Savages

kneeled down again and kissed the ground. Then, laying his head on the ground, he placed Robinson's foot firmly on top of his head. This was his way of swearing to be Robinson's slave forever.

Robinson lifted him up and patted him on the shoulder. Just then, the first savage, who had only been knocked out, began to move. Robinson pointed to him, and the native spoke some words which Robinson could not understand. Yet, the words sounded pleasant to Robinson's ears, for they were the first sounds of a man's voice that he had heard, except his own, in twenty-five years.

But there was no time for enjoying voices now, for the savage was already sitting up. The native pointed to the sword hanging from Robinson's belt. Robinson pulled it out and handed it to him. No sooner was the sword in his hand than he ran to his enemy and, with one blow, cut his head off.

The Native Swears His Loyalty.

When the job was done, the native returned to Robinson and laid the sword at his feet. Then he went over to the savage Robinson had shot. He looked at the dead body with a puzzled expression. Robinson understood that this fellow was wondering how he could have killed the savage from such a distance without touching him.

Robinson nodded his permission, and the native turned the body over and examined both sides. The small hole in the chest made him shake his head in wonder. Robinson would explain later, but for now, both men had to be buried so they wouldn't be found by the rest of their group.

Once that was done, Robinson led the native back to his fortress. There, he gave him food and water and made a place for the tired young man to lie down. Within minutes, the poor creature was sound asleep.

The Native Is Puzzled.

Robinson Admires His New Friend.

Chapter 9
Friday

Robinson stood staring at the sleeping young man. He was a handsome fellow, tall and well-built. Robinson guessed him to be about twenty-six years of age. His long, straight, black hair framed a round, plump face that, even while he slept, had a softness about it.

No more than half an hour had passed before the young man awoke and came running out of the cave to where Robinson was busy milking his goats. He laid his head on the ground and placed Robinson's foot upon his head as he had done before. Again, the man was showing his loyalty, promising to be Robinson's slave forever.

And so began a new life for Robinson Crusoe and the young native he named Friday. For, according to the calendar post Robinson had been keeping for twenty-five years, it was a Friday when he had saved the man's life.

That very night, Robinson taught Friday his name and also to call him "Master." Next, he taught Friday the words "yes" and "no" and what they meant.

Robinson gave the naked young man some clothes to wear so that he would be dressed in the same goatskin pants, jacket, and hat as his master. This pleased Friday very much, although he felt clumsy and uncomfortable in clothes at first.

The next morning, Robinson and Friday climbed to the top of the hill to look around

Friday is Pleased with His New Clothes.

for the cannibals. There was no sign of them or of their canoes. They had left without even bothering to search for their two companions.

Later in the day, when Robinson and Friday passed the spot where the two cannibals were buried, Friday made a sign to show that he wanted to dig them up and eat them. At this, Robinson got very angry and pretended to vomit at the thought of it. He called Friday away from the spot, and the young man obeyed. Robinson knew that he would have to put an end to the cannibal ways Friday had learned from his people.

Together, they headed for the beach and gathered up the remains of the cannibals feast. They burned everything to ashes.

As the days went by, Robinson learned that Friday was a faithful, loving, honest servant who loved him in the same way a child loves his father. Robinson was delighted with this and taught Friday everything he needed to

Burning the Remains of the Cannibals' Feast

know to help his master.

But the most important skill for Friday to learn was language. He had to learn to speak English and understand everything Robinson said. Friday proved to be a very bright student who enjoyed his lessons. He learned quickly and he learned well.

A year went by, then two. Robinson's life had become easier and happier with Friday as his friend and servant. If only he felt safe from the danger of an attack by the cannibals, Robinson would never want to leave his island ever again.

Friday's English had become so good that he was able to answer many of the questions Robinson had wondered about over the years. Friday had been to this island many times before with his people for feasts, so he knew all about the sea and the currents. He told of one strong current from the mainland. Robinson was to discover much later that this was

Robinson Teaches Friday English.

where the mighty Orinoco River of South America emptied into the Caribbean Sea not too far from the island.

Friday told Robinson about his country, his people, the sea, the coast, and the nations nearby. He also told Robinson that far to the west of his nation lived "much white beard mans like you, Master." For Robinson had great white whiskers which he kept neatly trimmed.

Robinson figured that the white men Friday referred to were Spaniards who had settled in some parts of South America. They might be the answer to his escape from the island.

When Robinson asked if it was possible to leave the island and find these white men, Friday answered, "Yes, yes, in two canoe."

At first, Robinson didn't understand what "two canoe" meant, but Friday soon explained it meant a large boat, as big as

Friday Tells About His Country.

two canoes.

As Friday began to understand more and more English, Robinson told him about his own life and how he had come to the island. He described how he lived in England, how people behaved there, how they traded with other parts of the world, and how they worshipped God.

After Robinson had described the wreck of his own ship, he took Friday out to see the lifeboat from his ship. It lay in ruins in the exact spot where it had washed up on shore twenty-seven years ago.

Friday studied the lifeboat for a while, then said, "Me see such boat like this come to my nation. Boat full of white mans. We save white mans from drown."

"How many white men were there?" asked Robinson. Friday held his fingers up again and again until he had reached the total of seventeen.

Friday Has Seen a Lifeboat Like This.

"What has become of them?" asked Robir son.

"They live," said Friday. "They live at m nation."

"If the men came in a lifeboat," said Robir son, "they must have been in a shipwreck Perhaps it was the shipwreck that took plac out on our rocks. The strong current migh have pulled them towards the mainlan where they landed at your nation."

"White mans with Friday's people one, tw three, four years," explained Friday.

"Why didn't your people kill and eat them" asked Robinson.

"They make brother with them," said Fr day, meaning that they had made a truc Then he added, "My nation no eat mans ex cept when fight war. Friday in war for ne king when Friday captured and brough here."

Robinson wondered if perhaps the your

White Men Came to Friday's People.

man secretly wished to be back with his people, so he asked, "Friday, do you wish to be in your own country again?"

Friday nodded and smiled. "I be much glad to be at my own nation."

"What would you do there?" asked Robinson. "Would you turn wild and eat man's flesh again? Would you be a savage as you were before?"

Friday shook his head and looked upset. "No, no!" he cried, "Friday tell peoples to live good, tell them pray God, tell them eat corn bread, cattle flesh, milk. No eat mans again."

"But won't they kill you for that?" asked Robinson.

"No, they no kill me. They willing to learn. They learn much from white beard mans that come in boat."

"Then you will go back?" asked Robinson.

Friday smiled, then answered, "Me no can swim that far."

"Friday No Eat Mans Again."

"But what if I made a canoe for you?" asked Robinson.

"Then Friday go," he answered, "but only if master go too."

"But if I go," protested Robinson, "they will kill me and eat me."

"No, no!" exclaimed Friday. "Me make sure they no eat you. Me make them much love you. Me tell them how you kill enemies and save Friday's life. You teachee me good. You teachee them good."

So Robinson took Friday to the other side of the island and showed him the small canoe he had hidden there many years ago.

"Well, Friday, shall we go to your nation?" asked Robinson.

"Boat too small go so far," he said.

So Robinson then took him to see his very first boat—the large canoe which was too heavy and too far inland to get to the water.

"That good big," said Friday, "but not good

"Boat Too Small Go So Far."

go on water."

"Yes, Friday," agreed Robinson. "This canoe has been lying here for twenty-three years. The sun has dried it and split it apart. It is too rotted to be used. But we can make ourselves a new one."

So Robinson and Friday set out to find a large tree to use for their canoe. This time, Robinson made certain to find a tree near the creek, so he wouldn't have a problem getting it into the water.

Working together, Robinson and Friday had the canoe finished in a month. But as close as they were to the creek, it still took another two weeks to move it there inch by inch on rollers.

Then Robinson cut down a straight young cedar tree for a mast and another smaller one to shape into a rudder for steering. He showed Friday how to shape the poles to fit, then set about making the sails himself.

Building a New Big Boat

Whatever pieces of old sails he had left were now twenty-seven years old and badly rotted. But Robinson found two pieces that were not as bad as the rest. So he went to work stitching them together. The sails took him nearly two months to finish.

Once the sails were tied to the mast and the rudder was in place, Robinson was ready for the boat's first big test.

Friday watched in amazement as Robinson steered the boat in every direction by moving the rudder. Friday only knew how to paddle a canoe to make it move, but he learned to sail as quickly as he learned everything else.

It was now the twenty-seventh anniversary of Robinson's arrival on the island. For the first time in all those years, he had great hopes for his escape before another year was notched out on his calendar.

Friday Watches Robinson Steer.

Preparing Food for the Voyage

Chapter 10
The Cannibals Return

The rainy season started just as the boat as finished, so Robinson decided to wait a onth or two before they set off on their voy- ;e. Besides, they needed that time to pre- ire for it. Bread had to be baked; meat had be dried; grapes had to be gathered; and nmunition had to be packed.

One day, while Robinson was busying him- lf with these tasks, Friday came running to m from the shore where he had been gath- ing turtle eggs.

"Master! O Master!" he cried, "O sorrow!

O bad!"

"What's the matter?" asked Robinson.

"Out yonder, there!" cried Friday, pointin to the sea. "One, two, three canoe. They con for Friday. They cut Friday in little piec and eat him."

"We will fight together, Friday," said Robi son. "I will defend you if you will stand by n and defend me."

"O Master," sobbed Friday, "me fight, n shoot, me die when you tell me die."

"Thank you, my friend," said Robinson a he took his spyglass and climbed up the sic of the hill. The glass quickly revealed twent one savages and three prisoners in thr canoes. They were landing on the shore ju below Robinson's hill where a thicket of tre ended on the beach.

Robinson climbed down and picked up h shotguns, muskets, and pistols. He called Friday, "Follow close behind me, but do n

More Savages and Prisoners Arrive.

do anything until I give the orders!"

When they reached the middle of the woods, they hid behind a large tree and looked out. The savages were sitting around the fire, already eating the flesh of one of their prisoners. Another prisoner lay tied up on the sand nearby.

"Look, Master!" whispered Friday, pointing to the prisoner on the sand. "See white beard man! Is one of white mans who come my nation in boat."

Robinson raised his spyglass for a better look. "Yes, Friday," he exclaimed, "it is a white man! He's wearing clothes."

Robinson was enraged. He motioned to Friday, and together they moved quietly to a tree closer to the edge of the thicket. They didn't have a moment to lose, for two of the savages had just left the group at the fire and were heading towards the white man. Their huge wooden swords were raised, ready

"It Is a White Man."

to cut him apart for their feast.

"Now, Friday," whispered Robinson, "do exactly as you see me do!"

Robinson raised his musket, took aim, and fired. At the same moment, Friday fired as well. Robinson's shot killed one savage and wounded two. Friday had taken better aim and he killed two and wounded three more.

The remaining savages jumped to their feet, but did not know which way to look or to run. They had no way of knowing where this death and destruction had come from.

Friday kept his eyes glued to Robinson waiting for further orders. Robinson dropped his musket and picked up his shotgun. Friday did the same.

"Fire!" cried Robinson.

Their shotguns had been loaded with small pistol bullets which spread in every direction when fired. So, even though they only killed two savages, they wounded many others. The

"Fire!"

savages, now covered with their own blood, ran about yelling and screaming like mad creatures.

"Now, Friday, bring your other musket and follow me!" called Robinson as he rushed out of the woods.

As soon as the savages saw them, they fell to the ground in fear. Five, however, jumped up and fled in terror towards the sea. Friday began firing at them just as they reached their canoes. All five fell.

Meanwhile, Robinson ran towards the prisoner who was still tied up on the beach. He pulled out his knife and cut the man's ropes. Then, lifting up the terrified man, Robinson asked him in Portuguese who he was.

The man was so weak and faint that he could not stand or speak. Robinson took a small bottle of rum from his pouch and gave the man a sip.

When some of his strength returned, the

Robinson Frees the White Man.

man answered Robinson's question. *"Espagnol,"* he said. ("Spaniard")

Robinson tried to explain, in the little Spanish he knew, that they would talk afterwards. But for now, they had to fight.

The man slowly explained that he had enough strength to fight and took the pistol and sword Robinson offered him. The feel of weapons in his hands seemed to give the man new strength. He flew at the savages and cut two of them to pieces with the sword.

Then another savage came at the Spaniard swinging his great wooden sword. The Spaniard, who was as brave as anyone Robinson had ever seen, fought the savage a long while. He landed two cuts on the savage's head. Then the savage, who was bigger and stronger than he, threw him down and tried to tear the sword out of his hand.

Robinson grabbed for his shotgun and started to run towards the downed man. But

The Spaniard Fights Bravely.

in an instant, the brave fellow managed to pull the pistol from his belt and shot the savage in the head.

By the time all the fighting was over, seventeen of the savages had been killed. The four who survived were already in a canoe, paddling furiously out to sea.

Friday dashed to the shore, calling, "We follow, we follow. No let savages go back nation. No let them come back with many hundred others."

Robinson agreed and jumped into one of the canoes. There, to his amazement, he found another prisoner, a native, with his arms and legs bound.

Robinson cut him free and called Friday over to explain to the frightened man that he had been rescued. Friday got into the boat, then stopped dead. He could not believe his eyes!

Another Prisoner!

"It My Father! It My Father!"

Chapter 11
Two Visitors

"It my father! It my father!" cried Friday as he hugged and kissed the man Robinson had just freed.

The man was almost dead with fear, for he had been tied up in the bottom of the boat and had no way of knowing what had been going on. He only heard the loud bursts of gunfire and the terrified screams of the savages.

Tears rolled down the man's face as his son held him close and began to massage his arms and legs. They were stiff and numb

159

from having been tied up for many days.

Robinson offered the man a drink of rum and a bunch of raisins. Friday gently put the bottle up to his lips, then fed him the fruit, piece by piece.

The discovery of Friday's father had turned Robinson's attention away from the escaping savages. By the time he remembered them, their canoe was out of sight.

The Spaniard, meanwhile, was resting under a tree. When Robinson returned to him, the man looked up with tears of thanks. Robinson lifted the weakened man up on his shoulder and carried him down to the beach. Then he gently placed him in the canoe beside Friday's father.

Robinson and Friday picked up the oars and began paddling along the shore. When they reached the creek close to Robinson's fortress, they docked the canoe. Then they carried the two men up to their home and

Robinson Helps the Spaniard.

placed them on two straw mattresses to rest.

While Robinson was preparing some food for their two visitors, Friday took the canoe and returned to the beach. He buried all the dead savages and the remains of their bloody feast.

When Friday returned, the four men sat in the cave and talked. As Robinson spoke, Friday translated his words into the language of the natives. The Spaniard was able to understand it for he had been living with the natives for four years.

They discussed what might happen when the four escaped savages returned to their people. Friday's father pointed outside to the storm that had come up and explained that he didn't think the savages could survive such a storm in their small canoe. The Spaniard added that if they did survive, they would probably be blown far south of the shore where they lived.

Friday Translates Robinson's Words.

Friday reminded them all that if the savages did manage to reach their own shore safely, they probably would have been so frightened from the noise and fire of the guns, they would blame it on their evil spirits. They probably also would swear that the two creatures who attacked them, Robinson and Friday, had been sent by the spirits to destroy them.

Friday's father agreed. He said that he had heard the four savages cry out about the spirits as they were paddling away. To them, no man could shoot fire. And no man could kill another from so far away.

Robinson was to find out years later that these four savages did, indeed, return home safely. But, neither they nor their fellow tribesmen ever dared set foot on the "enchanted" island again, for fear that the fire from the gods would destroy them.

However, at the time, Robinson did not

The Savages Paddled Away in Fear.

know this. So, for a long while, he was in constant fear that the savages would return. Therefore, he was always on his guard.

As Friday's father and the Spaniard recovered their strength, Robinson began to think more and more about his original plan to leave the island. Friday's father assured him that the natives in his tribe would welcome Robinson. The Spaniard was eager to leave too, for his own men were badly in need of food and other provisions. They were at the mercy of the savages and didn't know, from one minute to the next, whether or not the savages would turn on them. These fourteen surviving Spaniards on the mainland had no way of escaping, since they had no boat and no tools to build one.

When Robinson suggested helping them escape, the Spaniard swore that all his men would be grateful to Robinson all their lives. They would do anything Robinson asked if he

Making Plans to Leave the Island

was able to rescue them.

So Robinson decided to send Friday's father and the Spaniard across to the mainland to get them. But the Spaniard suggested that they wait six months before starting out on the voyage. That way, there would be time to grow more food to take care of the fourteen extra men they would be bringing back. And also, Robinson and Friday would have the help of two extra pairs of hands to plow the ground and harvest the crops.

The Spaniard's advice was so good and so wise that Robinson agreed immediately. The four men set to work farming the land, baking bread, drying grapes, and preserving meat.

At the end of six months, everything was ready for the voyage. The Spaniard knew how to operate the sails and rudder on Robinson's canoe, and Friday's father learned it quickly.

168

Harvesting Extra Crops

Robinson gave both men muskets and gun powder, but warned them to use their arm only in an emergency. He also gave them a eight-day supply of food and water—enoug to last them on their trip to the mainlan and on their return trip to the island.

As Robinson said good-bye to the Spaniar and Friday's father, they arranged for th Spaniard to fire his musket twice upon h return to the island. That way, Robinso would know that friends were coming ashor

It was now twenty-eight years and tw months, according to the notches on Robi son's calendar post. Everything seemed to l pointing to a speedy rescue from the island!

Setting Sail

"Master, Master! They Are Come!"

Chapter 12
Englishmen Reach the Island

One morning, eight days later, Robinson was awakened by Friday's calls.

"Master, Master!" he cried. "They are come, they are come!"

Robinson jumped up and ran from his tent. His eyes searched the sea and came upon a boat about three miles out. But the boat was *not* coming from the mainland.

"Come back, Friday!" he called. "These are not the people we are expecting. We do not know if they are friends or enemies."

Robinson immediately went for his

spyglass and climbed the hill with it. No
sooner had he reached the top than he saw a
ship lying at anchor about six miles to the
southeast. It appeared to be an English ship
and the smaller boat heading for shore was
its longboat, which is a small boat carried on
a merchant ship.

Robinson was overjoyed at the thought of
seeing a ship filled with his own countrymen.
But he was worried as well, for English ships
did not usually do any trading in this part of
the world. There had been no storms recently
to drive a ship here. So, Robinson decided to
keep himself hidden until he could discover
exactly why the ship had come.

As the longboat neared the shore, the tide
was coming in, so the sailors ran their boat
up on the beach. Robinson saw eleven men on
board, but three of them appeared to be tied
hand and foot.

The sailors jumped out of the boat and

Englishmen!

pulled their three prisoners out after them. Once on shore, they untied the men's ropes. One of the prisoners fell to his knees and appeared to be pleading with one of the sailors. The sailor pushed him back.

Friday, who also had been watching through a spyglass, called out, "O Master! You see English mans eat prisoner just like savage mans."

"No, Friday," answered Robinson. "While I do fear that they plan to murder their prisoners, you may be sure they will not eat them."

Robinson stood trembling at the thought of watching three Englishmen being murdered. He had to try to save them.

His chance came a few minutes later when six of the sailors ran off to explore the island. The three prisoners were left unguarded, except for two sailors drinking some rum in the longboat. But the prisoners had no place to

Will the English Prisoners Be Murdered?

flee, so they sat down under a tree at the edge of the woods and looked at each other in despair.

Robinson and Friday had seen enough. They climbed down from the hill and began loading their shotguns, muskets, and pistols. Then they filled their pouches with extra bullets and gunpowder.

Seeing that the six sailors had not returned and the other two were either asleep or drunk in the boat, Robinson and Friday headed down the hill towards the prisoners. They came up behind them quietly, and Robinson got their attention by calling softly, "Who are you, gentlemen?"

The men were startled, not only by the sound of a strange voice, but by Robinson's appearance as well. He looked very fierce in his goatskin clothes and with all the weapons in his arms. The men said nothing, but seemed ready to attack him.

The Prisoners Are Startled!

Then Robinson spoke again. "Gentlemen, do not be surprised at the sight of me. I am a friend, and perhaps I can help you."

"You must be an angel sent directly from Heaven," said one of the men. "But I fear no one can help us now."

Robinson smiled. "If God had sent an angel to help you," he explained, "that angel would have come better dressed. Please do not be afraid. I am an Englishman, and this is my man, Friday. We have arms and ammunition, so perhaps we can help."

One of the men stood up. "I was the captain of that ship anchored out there at sea," he explained. "My men staged a mutiny against me and took over my ship. At first they were going to murder me, but then they decided to set me ashore on this island with my first mate here and this other gentleman who was a passenger. We were convinced we would die here, for we never dreamed anyone

The Captain Describes the Mutiny.

lived on the island."

"Well, Friday and I do, but more of tha later," said Robinson, looking out towards th boat and then into the woods. "No one ha noticed us yet, but we dare not take an chances. Follow me quickly!"

Robinson led the men deeper into th woods. When they reached a safe hidde spot, Robinson turned to the captain an asked, "Sir, if I help you escape and get you ship back, are you willing to do two things fc me?"

"I will do anything you ask, sir. My shi and I will be yours to command. And I wi swear my loyalty to you for life." The othe two men nodded in agreement.

"That will be good," said Robinson, "bi you must also agree that while you are o this island, you will take orders from m And then, if we manage to recover your shi you must promise to carry me and my ma

Robinson Leads the Men into the Woods.

Friday back to England at no cost."

"You have my word," said the captain.

"Fine," said Robinson. "Now let us plan our next move against these mutineers."

The captain didn't want to kill any of his men if he could help it, but he also didn't want any of them to leave the island and warn the others on the ship.

Just as Robinson was about to answer him, they heard the sailors returning through the woods. Robinson gave each of his men a gun, and together they fell upon the sailors.

The first two were shot dead, and the others, seeing they were in danger, begged for mercy. The captain told them that he would spare their lives if they would promise to be loyal to him and help him recover the ship. The men swore their loyalty, and the captain believed them. He spared their lives, but at Robinson's insistence, he kept them bound hand and foot.

The Sailors Beg for Mercy.

The two sailors who had been in the boa
heard the shooting and ran into the woods
When they saw what had happened, they
surrendered and were tied up as well.

Robinson and Friday led the men back to
the fortress. They put the prisoners in the
cave and sat down to plan their next move.

"I don't know what we can possibly do,"
said the captain, "for there are still twenty
six men on board the ship. They know very
well that the punishment for mutiny is hang
ing. So they will fight savagely to keep from
being captured."

"I agree, sir," said Robinson, "they are des
perate men. And for the five of us to go
against twenty-six would be certain death for
us. No, no, we must find a better way. We
must surprise them in a trap!"

Hiding the Prisoners in the Cave

The Ship Signals the Longboat.

Chapter 13
Robinson Puts Down a Mutiny

"I think I have an idea," said the captain. "Surely more of the crew will come ashore in search of their shipmates. We can trap them first, then take the ship later."

At that moment, the ship's guns fired, and signal flags were raised on her mast. They were ordering the longboat to return to the ship. The guns fired again and again. But no boat stirred.

At last, another boat was lowered. Through his spyglass, Robinson saw ten sailors, armed with muskets, rowing towards shore. As they came closer, the captain recognized the men on board.

"Of the ten," he said, "three are very honest fellows. I am sure they were forced to join this mutiny. But the officer in charge and the rest of them are ugly, desperate men."

Robinson smiled confidently. "Sir," he said, "we are five men, plus two of the prisoners in the cave whom you trust. That adds up to seven. Surely we can deal with those ten, especially if we can count on the three who you say are honest men."

The captain agreed, so Robinson sent Friday into the cave to free the two prisoners. Once everyone was armed, Robinson led his army of five back down to the woods.

The boat had landed, and its crew was on shore. They were shouting with all their might, trying to locate their lost shipmates. They fired several shots, but received no answer. Finally, seven of the sailors headed

Another Longboat Heads for Shore.

up into the hills on their search, leaving three men to guard the boat.

Now, a new problem faced Robinson. If he captured the seven men on shore, the other three would surely flee back to their ship. Then the captain would never recover his ship, and Robinson's hopes for escape would be doomed.

Robinson thought a while, and then the answer came to him. He would separate the sailors on the island, bring the three guards on shore, and capture their boat.

He told Friday and two of the men to spread out in different directions on the island. When they reached a hill where their voices would carry, they were to call "Hello!" as loud as they could.

When the sailors answered, they were to call again and move further inland, heading towards the creek. The sailors would surely follow the voices, thinking it was their

Robinson Tells Friday His Plan.

shipmates calling.

Friday and his men spread out and soo had the sailors a mile from shore near th creek. Since the tide was high, the sailo couldn't get across, so they called to th guards to bring the boat around.

The three guards brought the boat into th creek and rowed their men across. Two of th guards remained behind with the boat, whi the third joined in the search.

This was exactly what Robinson had hope for. As soon as the sailors were out of sigh Robinson and his men attacked the two su prised guards. Seeing themselves outnun bered, they gave up immediately. The capta identified the guards as two of the hone men he had spoken of earlier. These me were happy to rejoin their captain and figh for him against the mutineers.

Friday and his men returned soon afte wards and reported their mission a comple

Two Honest Sailors Surrender.

success. They had led the sailors so far into the woods and had left them there so lost and so exhausted, that the sailors could not possibly return to the creek before dark. And darkness was all that Robinson needed to make his plan a success.

By nightfall, eight weary and complaining sailors trudged back to the shore of the creek. The boat was there, but their two guards were missing. The sailors ran in different directions, calling to their two missing shipmates. They were puzzled about this second disappearance.

Robinson and his men watched the sailors from their hiding places in the woods. When the leader of the mutiny approached the large rock where the captain was hiding, the captain jumped up and fired. The villainous mutineer fell dead on the spot.

Robinson regrouped his army, and they surrounded the rest of the sailors in the dark.

The Captain Shoots the Mutineer.

Robinson ordered one of his men to call to the sailors and try to talk them into surrendering.

"Tom Smith! Tom Smith!" called the man.

Smith answered immediately. "Is that you Williams?"

"Ay, ay! For God's sake, Smith, throw down your arms and surrender this minute or you will all be dead men!"

"Who must we surrender to?" called Smith. "And where are they?"

"Our captain is here with fifty men," said Williams. "We have been hunting you for two hours, and we have you surrounded. Your leader has been killed and I am a prisoner."

"Will they spare our lives if we surrender?" asked Smith.

The captain answered him. "Smith, you know my voice. If you lay down your arms immediately and surrender, your lives will be spared, that is, all except Will Atkins. Fo

"Surrender This Minute!"

him, there is no mercy."

Upon hearing this, Will Atkins cried out, "For God's sake, Captain, spare me too. What have I done that all these others have not done?"

"It was you who attacked me when the mutiny began, Atkins," said the captain. "I will have no mercy at all on you. Your only hope is that perhaps the governor of this island will have mercy and spare your life."

Robinson chuckled softly behind a tree. "Yes, I guess I am the governor of the island," he whispered to himself. But there was no time for enjoying his new title now. The sailors had laid down their arms, so Robinson sent three of his men to tie them up.

Since Robinson did not want his prisoners to know that he really didn't have an army of fifty men, he called to his army to stay hidden. Then he ordered the captain and his men to lead the prisoners back to the cave.

"I Guess I Am the Governor."

Robinson kept himself hidden too. It would not be wise for the prisoners to see a governor dressed in a goatskin cap and goatskin pants. "Let them think what they will about this mysterious governor," thought Robinson. "They will have time enough to see me when I decide their fate."

Once in the cave, the prisoners told the captain how sorry they were for the mutiny and begged him again to spare their lives.

"You are not my prisoners," explained the captain coldly. "You belong to the governor of this island who is an Englishman. The governor is the only one who can decide whether to hang you here or send you back to England to be tried and hanged there."

"But couldn't you speak to the governor for us?" begged one of the prisoners.

"I shall try," said the captain. "But the governor has already ordered that Will Atkins be hanged at daybreak."

"The Governor Can Hang You Here!"

Even though the captain had made up this entire story, it had the effect he had hoped for. Atkins fell to his knees and pleaded for his life. The others begged not to be sent back to England for they knew very well that hanging was the only punishment given any man who took part in a mutiny.

"The decision can only be made by His Excellency, the Governor," said the captain. "Right now, he sits in his castle on the other side of the island deciding your fate."

But His Excellency, the Governor, was standing outside the cave in the darkness milking his goats!

His Excellency, the Governor!

Making Plans to Seize the Ship

Chapter 14
Robinson Seizes the Ship

When the captain had finished talking to the prisoners in the cave, he rejoined Robinson outside. They had to make plans now for seizing the ship. Both men agreed that the seven men who made up their small army were not enough to overpower the rest of the mutineers on the ship.

So the captain went back inside the cave, hoping to pick out more men who could be trusted. He began by reminding them how lucky they were still to be alive. For surely they deserved to be hanged.

The prisoners nodded sadly, realizing that their captain spoke the truth.

"But," continued the captain, "if you join with me and help me recover my ship, I have the word of the governor that each of you will be pardoned."

The men were overjoyed at the chance to save their lives. They fell to their knees and swore to the captain that they would be faithful to him till their dying day.

"I shall go to the castle now," said the captain, "and tell the governor what you have promised."

The captain returned to Robinson's tent and reported the conversation. Robinson decided to use only five of the prisoners and leave the other six in the cave. That way, if the five did not keep their promises and fight loyally, the rest would be hanged.

When the captain reported this to the prisoners, they realized that the governor was a

A Chance to Save Their Lives

very hard man, but a wise one as well. For now the prisoners themselves had to persuade each other to fight bravely and loyally or risk being hanged.

Robinson and Friday stayed on shore to guard the remaining prisoners as the captain and his eleven men climbed into two boats. It was midnight, and the darkness would hide their true identities from the crew as they boarded. The mutineers would simply think the boats held their own men returning from shore.

Once on board, the captain and his men started the attack. They overpowered the men on deck and fastened the hatches to lock in those who were below.

Then they broke into the cabin of the mutineer who had taken over as captain. After much firing back and forth, the leader of the mutiny lay dead and the men around him wounded.

The Attack Begins.

Seeing their leader killed, the rest of the men surrendered. The mutiny was over, and the ship was now back in the true captain's hands.

The captain ordered seven guns to be fired as a signal to Robinson that the attack had been a success. After a two-hour wait on shore, Robinson was overjoyed.

At daybreak, the captain returned to the island. He embraced Robinson in his arms for a long while. Then, pointing to the ship, he said, "My dear friend and rescuer, there is your ship. She is all yours, and so am I and all of my men."

Robinson looked out. There, at the entrance to the creek, lay his ship. Her flags were flying, and her sails were spread. She was ready to carry him home.

Robinson could not utter a word. His joy left him speechless for several minutes. Then, finally, the tears came.

A Ship to Carry Robinson Home

Robinson took the captain's hand and sobbed, "My friend, you have truly been sent from Heaven to rescue me!" Then he fell to his knees and whispered a prayer of thanks to God.

To celebrate this joyous occasion, the captain had brought some gifts ashore for the governor. He called to his men to bring these up to the fortress. There were cases of wine, sacks of meat, boxes of biscuits, crates of vegetables, and suits of clothing, complete with shoes and stockings.

Robinson was delighted, especially with the clothing! But wearing it was another story. For it was rather uncomfortable putting on the sort of shirts, pants, hats, stockings, and shoes he had not worn for twenty-eight years.

After Robinson walked around a while to get used to his new clothes, he and the captain sat down to discuss what was to be done with the prisoners they had captured during

Gifts from the Captain

the attack on the ship. All but two had surrendered peacefully, but the two who hadn't could be a problem.

"We can take them back to England in irons," said the captain, "but I fear that they will still make trouble aboard ship."

"Then why not leave them here on the island?" suggested Robinson. "Surely they can survive just as I did."

When the captain agreed, Robinson had Friday bring the two men to him. Dressed in his new clothing, Robinson looked every bit as impressive as the governor of an island should look.

As the prisoners entered, Robinson studied them long and hard. "I have been told all about your evil deeds by my friend, the captain," began Robinson. "I know how you ran away with his ship and were planning to attack and rob other ships as well. But you will be punished, just as your leader has been

The Governor Punishes the Mutineers.

punished. Look out to your ship, you villain
See your leader hanging dead from the tip
the yardarm! What have you mutineers
say for yourselves? Shall I execute you a
pirates? As governor, I have the right to a
so, you know!"

One of the men answered, "Your Exce
lency, we ask for mercy."

"Well," said Robinson, "I do not know wh
mercy I can show you, for I plan to leave th
island with all my men. I am going to En
land with the captain. And the only way yc
could go along would be as prisoners in iron
Then, once we reach England, you will ha
to stand trial for mutiny. And the result
that, you surely know, is hanging. So, I real
do not know what is best for you, unless yc
wish to try living here on the island by you
selves. I would not care since I am leaving."

"Oh, thank you, Your Excellency," cried tl
men. They both certainly preferred to stay a

One Mutineer Hangs from the Yardarm.

the island rather than be taken to England to be hanged. And since Robinson didn't really want any more killings at this point, he agreed to let them stay.

Once the men were freed from their ropes, Robinson spent the next several hours explaining to them how he had survived for twenty-eight years on the island. He showed them how he built his fortress, how he plowed his ground, how he planted his crops, how he ground his corn, how he made his earthenware pots, how he wove baskets, how he dried his grapes, how he baked his bread, how he milked his goats, and how he made butter and cheese. In all, he told them everything they needed to know in order to survive on the island.

He also told them of the Spaniards who were to arrive on the island shortly, and he made the two men promise to treat the new arrivals kindly.

Robinson Explains How to Survive.

Robinson also left them all his arms and promised them extra ammunition from the ship before she sailed.

So Robinson spent his last night on the island walking along the paths and climbing the hills he had come to know so well over the years.

The next morning, the captain sent a boat ashore for Robinson and Friday. As Robinson prepared to leave, he carried with him his great goatskin cap, his goatskin umbrella, his parrot, and all the gold and silver that had lain in the cave, growing rusty and tarnished over the years.

And so, according to the notches on his calendar post, Robinson left his island on the 19th of December, in the year 1686. It was exactly twenty-eight years, two months, and nine days after he had arrived!

Robinson Leaves His Island.

Robinson and Friday Arrive in England.

Chapter 15
Home Again

After a long voyage of six months at sea, Robinson arrived back in England on the 11th of June, in the year 1687. He had been gone for thirty-five years.

He went immediately to his home in Yorkshire, but found that his mother and father had been dead for many years. However, he did locate two of his sisters and the sons of his brother who had also died.

During the next seven years, Robinson traveled between England and Portugal, trying to settle the business affairs of his plantation in

Brazil. The plantation had become quite successful, and the honest men Robinson had left in charge of it had managed it wisely. There was a great deal of money put aside for Robinson, and he arranged for it to be sent to him in England.

He thought many times about returning to Brazil to live, but then decided against it. He sold the plantation to two of his neighbors there and settled in England.

Robinson had taken into his care the two sons of his dead brother. One of the young men was studying law, but the other seemed to have inherited Robinson's desire for a life at sea.

Robinson arranged for him to go to work on a ship, and, after five years, the lad proved himself to be a bold seaman and a successful trader. So Robinson outfitted a ship for him, and another Crusoe became a merchant trader.

Robinson's Two Nephews

After the young man had returned from several successful trading voyages to Spain he persuaded Robinson to join him on his next voyage. This one was to be to South America.

Robinson couldn't resist the thrill of a new adventure. He and Friday had been on land now for eight years.

On this voyage, Robinson revisited his island. He was eager to learn what had become of the two prisoners he had left there and the Spaniards who had been expected. He found the Englishmen and the Spaniards living together in peace. They were, in fact, farming and colonizing the island.

It seems that five of the Spaniards had returned once to the mainland and rescued eleven men and five women from the savages. So, by the time Robinson arrived on the island, there were about twenty young children running about.

Return to the Island.

Robinson stayed on the island for a month. He gave the people fresh supplies of arms, gunpowder, clothing, and tools. And he left two workmen there—a carpenter and blacksmith.

When Robinson's ship landed in Brazil afterwards, he sent another ship back to the island with cows, sheep, and hogs. He also sent seven women as wives for some of the men.

In the years that followed, Robinson and Friday returned to the island several times, each time bringing more and more supplies to the colonists. But, even though each new voyage was an adventure itself, the most thrilling adventure Robinson Crusoe would ever have in his lifetime was the adventure of twenty-eight years as governor of his very own island.

A New Colony Grows!

1. Spritsail
2. Spritsail topsail
3. Foresail
4. Fore topsail
5. Fore topgallant
6. Fore royal
7. Mainsail
8. Main topsail
9. Main topgallant
10. Main royal
11. Mizzen topsail
12. Mizzen topgallant
13. Mizzen

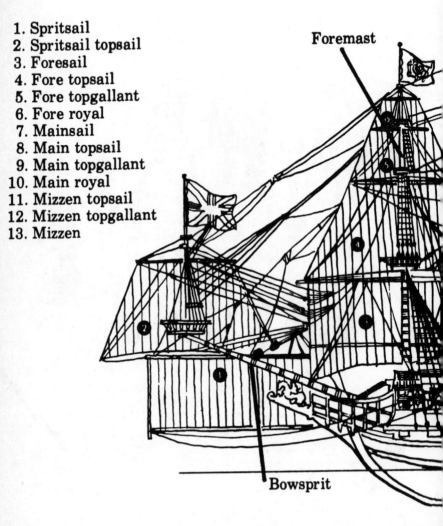

Foremast

Bowsprit

Three-Masted Sailing Ship

Mainmast

Mizzenmast

...om Robinson Crusoe's Day